RORY'S HECKIN' GRUMPY DAY

THIS BOOK IS DEDICATED TO ALL OF RORY'S AMAZING FANS AND FOLLOWERS! THANK YOU ALL FOR YOUR SUPPORT AND ENCOURAGEMENT!

PHOTO BY
MARSHIE'S ROAR PET PHOTOGRAPHY

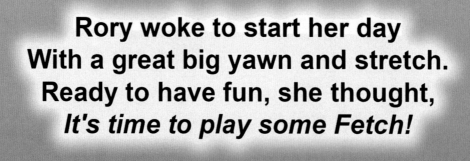

Rory woke to start her day
With a great big yawn and stretch.
Ready to have fun, she thought,
It's time to play some Fetch!

Where's my ball? she wondered.
Rory was a bit confused.
She searched but couldn't find it.
She was highly unamused.

Rory looked around the room.
It was like it disappeared.
"Oh yeah! I might remember!
I'll check ONE last spot!" she cheered.

She wasn't badly injured,
And her head would be okay,
But that was just the start of
Rory's heckin' grumpy day.

She checked outside the window.
She inspected everywhere,
But all she saw was blankets.
She thought nothing else was there.

Rory tiptoed toward the couch
She slowly stepped by Terror.
She still saw only blankets...
He sprung and leapt to scare her!

She wandered to the kitchen
To prepare a yummy snack.
She felt like she deserved it
For that brutal cat attack.

Rory looked inside the fridge,
But none of her snacks were there.
All of the drawers were empty.
Every single shelf was bare.

With a sad and empty belly,
Rory searched around the floor.
She found one tiny crumb,
But her search turned up no more.

"This won't fill up my tummy!"
She shouted as it rumbled.
"And my head still kind of hurts
From when I tripped and tumbled!"

She grumped, and barked, and cried
As she flailed around the couch.

Biting cushions, biting pillows,
Rory was a total grouch!

"You've had it rough," said Terror,
"But that's really no excuse."
Rory snapped, "I'm done today!
It's been nothing but ABOOSE!"

"Think of all you're grateful for,"
Terror stated with a grin.
"Come! Let's go play Hide and Seek.
I might even let you win!"

She thought over what he said,
And she knew he might be right.
She really did get joy from
Basking in that warm sunlight.

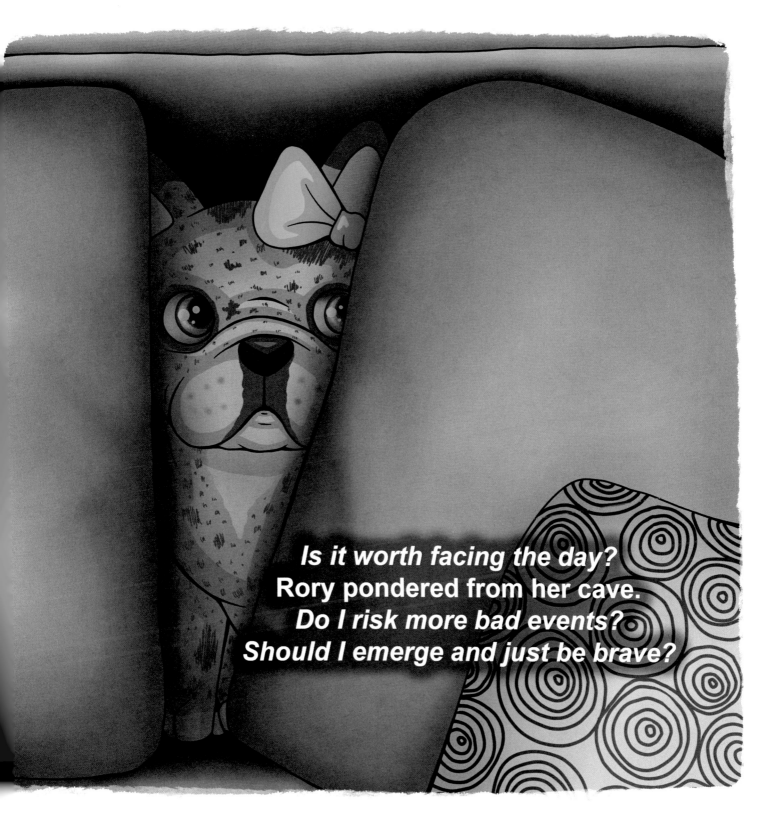

Is it worth facing the day?
Rory pondered from her cave.
Do I risk more bad events?
Should I emerge and just be brave?

Rory peeked out from her fort,
And she poked out just one paw.
To her surprise and her delight,
She was stunned by what she saw!

A plate of chicken nuggets
(Nuggies are her favorite food)!
"WOW! These nuggies are so good!
This really helps my grumpy mood!"

RORY THE FRENCHIE

PHOTO BY UNLEASHED WITH LOVE

Rory is an adorable, sassy French bulldog. She is known for throwing tantrums, making couch forts, losing costume contests, and having a crush on a certain celebrity.

She brings a smile to everyone who meets her and spreads joy to her fans every single day. She makes life better for everyone who knows her.

Everything in this book was inspired by Rory's life, and of course, we had to include her famous catch phrases: "heckin' pupset" and "aboose"! We also couldn't leave out Rory's cat brother, Terror. Terror is a 10 year old tabby, and he really does act like an older brother to her.

I hope you get to know Rory's funny, unique personality through this book. I also hope it reminds you that it's okay to be grumpy sometimes, but don't let a bad day stop you from appreciating the things you enjoy, especially chicken nuggies!!

Made in United States
Orlando, FL
15 April 2024

45820120R00020